reassigned 6/08
11 x
10/00
12 x
9/08

c.10

The Wonderful Chirrionera and Other Tales from Mexican Folklore

THE WONDERFUL CHIRRIONERA
AND OTHER TALES FROM MEXICAN FOLKLORE

WOODCUTS BY BARBARA MATHEWS WHITEHEAD
SELECTED AND EDITED BY DAVID L. LINDSEY

Heidelberg Publishers, Inc. • Austin, Texas • 1974

The tales in this book were originally printed in *Puro Mexicano* published by the Texas Folklore Society in 1935 and edited by J. Frank Dobie. Though the stories as printed here have undergone some few editorial changes in an effort to render them more readily understood by children, they are essentially the same.

Recognition is due Riley Aiken for his original recounting of "The Three Counsels" ("Three Bits of Advice"), "A Boom in Guarache Leather" ("Sandal Leather"), and "Charge This to the Hat", and to Dan Storm for "The Wonderful Chirrionera".

And preeminent recognition is due the *gente* of Mexico who demonstrate so artfully the ageless charm of storytelling.

Copyrighted © 1974 by Heidelberg Publishers, Inc., Austin, Texas
All rights reserved
Standard Book Number: 0-913206-03-2
Printed in the United States of America
Designed by Barbara Mathews Whitehead

For
ANTHONY *and* RACHEL
May they always, in some part,
remain children.

THE WONDERFUL CHIRRIONERA

Many strange things happen in this old world, my friend, as you well know. And one of the strangest things I have ever heard is the story of old Mariano and the wonderful chirrionera.

Now many people do not believe this story, but I will tell it to you and you can judge for yourself. It is said that if you go to old Mariano's house today and look him in the eyes and say the word "chirrionera" you will see that the old man's brows will come down over his eyes so he cannot see, and his moustache will droop over his mouth to shut in the words. Up around his ears he will pull his sarape; and you may shout at him and wave your hands in front of his face all day if you like, and he will remain so.

Very strange you say? Well listen to the story:

Old Mariano had next to his house a garden and an orchard, the most beautiful and luxuriant imaginable, surrounded by a high adobe wall. Above the wall could be seen the peaches shining in the sun, and the plums red and sparkling like rubies, and so many of them. Many! Many! You could not see the branches. The same of grapes, mangoes, limes, and oranges. Such fruits! The people passing by would stop and stare and swallow as if they were eating. Ah, so delicious and so plentiful, it makes me hungry to think of them now.

And Mariano, quick-tempered, irritable old bachelor that he was, smiled never so broadly as when people would stop to gaze in hunger at his fruits. The few times he was known to laugh were when three little boys who lived nearby would come to gaze up pitifully at the ripe fruits. Juan, José, and Daniel, the boys were called; and when they went over to old Mariano's house, he would point up to his fruits and say: "Ah, you admire my fruit, boys! And well you might. They are even more delicious than they look. Ah, see how the blackbirds and doves eat them greedily! Is this not proof enough that the fruits are most delicious? Ah, and see how that biggest blackbird goes from mango to plum just tasting, tasting daintily."

And the three little brothers, Juan, José, and Daniel, from down below on the ground, looking up, would say one to the other, "Just look at the peaches, the plums, the little mangoes, and the little grapes! Why can not we taste of that mango that the blackbird has just knocked to the ground inside?"

But old Mariano would show his wolf teeth and laugh.

No, never would old Mariano give even a partly rotten fruit to anyone. In fact, if a blackbird should alight on an overhanging branch and peck a fruit outside to the ground so that the three brothers could pick it up, devouring it among themselves as they ran, the old man would get his rifle, shoot at the guilty blackbird, and then spend the rest of the day talking angrily to himself. Yet he knew that the three brothers were the sons of Juan Santos, a poor mule herder who worked hard every day, only oftentimes to spend all his hard-earned and scanty wages on tequila Saturday night, so that some days there were neither tortillas nor frijoles in the house.

But as time passed, the three boys grew taller and their bones harder, while old Mariano began to stoop more as he lifted his feet more slowly from one step to the next. Time is just.

At last one day the three brothers tasted of the jealously-guarded fruits of old Mariano. Early one morning before the dawn Juan, José, and Daniel went down the hill to the creek; and here, working like ants with their machetes, they cut a long pole and made little steps in it so that soon they had a chicken-ladder like those you see going from one landing to the other in mines. After much stopping to rest, the three carried the ladder up the hill and slowly, slowly over to old Mariano's orchard. Grunting and panting, they managed to place the small end of their ladder upon the top of the high adobe wall. The youngest brother, Daniel, who did not wear sandals, went quietly, quietly, his bare feet making no more noise on the ground than those of a coyote, up to Old Mariano's door and peeked in. Back he came with the word that the miserable old man was taking his afternoon siesta and was trumpeting snores so loud that surely he would not be awakened if two burros were suddenly to bray into each of his ears.

Like a squirrel, Juan, the eldest brother, went up the ladder. From the wall top he climbed into a peach tree. His hands working as rapidly as those of a young monkey, he snatched fruits in every direction and let them fall over the outside of the wall to José and Daniel, who threw them into sacks slung about their necks in readiness.

When their sacks were nearly full of fruit, the boys began to relax their caution and to laugh. In this moment old Mariano appeared in his door-way. Yelling insanely and swearing, he threw his hands at the sky and broke running toward the boys. Daniel and José with their sacks turned and raced into the chaparral and took straight up the mountainside like two young goats who know that the wolf is behind them. Juan hardly had time to scramble down the ladder. Just as he reached the ground, old Mariano, rushing up like a bull, made a grab at the boy and took hold of the one suspender to his pants. Juan jerked away, leaving the old man holding the strip of blue cloth in his hand. Then old Mariano gave chase; but Juan, even though he had to hold up his pants as he ran, soon left the puffing old man behind.

Bellowing curses into the unoffending air and stamping the innocent ground, old Mariano went, not to his own house, but, as do all his kind in cases like this, to the house of the boys' parents. Here he awaited Juan Santos and asked him indignantly what kind of vicious creatures he had raised for sons, that they must rob an old man. In the jail, the jail, was where they belonged. They would surely be executed when they grew up, all of them.

"I am sorry," said Juan Santos, "but every day before the dawn I get my mules together and when the sun comes up I am driving the animals over the trails through the mountains. Already darkness has come when I arrive here at the house. How can I know what my sons are doing during the day? I cannot tie them as I would dogs, for they know how to untie the knots. Neither can I put them in a corral as I would goats, for they would very quickly climb over and be out. But this I tell you: every time they steal your fruit, I shall let you whip them, as punishment."

"Very well," said old Mariano. "It is good."

Juan Santos told his boys what he had said to their enemy. "But," he added, "that old man is too weak. He cannot hurt you. He will only drive some of the dust out of your clothes."

So the next time the boys stole fruit from old Mariano's orchard, Juan Santos took his boys over to the old man's house. With a small stick, the old man first worked on Juan, the eldest, who shouted, "Ay! ay!" at each blow as if his end had come. By the time the old man was ready for José, the strength was gone from his arm. But José yelled mightily. When finally it came Daniel's turn, his cries were plainly artificial ones, for the old man could hardly lift his arm for the blow.

Little did old Mariano realize how many years had stolen into his bones, stiffening his joints and weakening his muscles. Daily came the boys to his orchard, and reported faithfully for their punishment, crying loudly, loudly.

Old Mariano was desperate.

"Ah, poor me," Mariano said, "at first I chopped to pieces the ladders of the little devils; but they make new ones. Chihuahua! I cannot keep up with them. They are three and I am one. Oh, yes, they still come to be whipped. But, with them it is a playful game and with me hard work beyond my years. Loudly they shout and cry when I whip them; but I know that in truth, even while they yell so loudly, they are at me laughing. Poor me! Poor me! I do not know what to do. What can I do? Must I continue suffering injustice from three young fiends? Ah, if only again I had my youth, my strength. Poor me! What ill luck has befallen me!"

His bad luck caused old Mariano to arise very early one morning. The night before, much tequila had made him fall asleep early; and as he had not cursed all he desired that day, he arose early this morning so as to spend every bit of the day in the thing that now was his only pastime and consolation.

He had not been seated outside his doorway long, when suddenly, becoming alert, he did something he never before had been known to do. He became suddenly silent in the very middle of an eloquent sentence of swearing, leaving half the curse to float uncompleted in the air.

With open mouth, he stared out in front of his house at the road where an oxcart was passing. The driver lay in the cart sleeping peacefully; but the two oxen went on at a very good pace. Why? A whip would strike out from time to time, hitting the oxen a smart blow. Mariano blinked his old eyes. Surely he couldn't be still drunk from the tequila of last night! A whip striking the oxen! Yet no one holding the handle! Thus it was.

"Hey there, wait!" Leaping up from his chair like a man truly inspired with the devil, Mariano went running, stumbling, yelling, and waving his arms for the driver to stop. As the old man approached, the driver sat up and rubbed his eyes.

"What a strange whip you have, sir!" old Mariano panted.

"You think so?" answered the driver, smiling.

"No handle, and no hand ahold of it; yet it strikes the oxen. Are you perhaps a magician . . . ?"

As the cart came to a halt, the whip curled up like a snake. Mariano's eyes almost popped from their sockets. The whip was a snake! For a moment the old man was speechless.

"Yes," said the driver calmly, "many wonder at my Chapo. He is a chirrionera, one of those snakes who stand upon their heads and whip their enemies. I have trained him to keep the oxen going at a steady pace."

By this time Mariano had managed to loosen his tongue. Now his eyes shone with a new fire — like those of a fox who has suddenly thought of a new and better way to catch chickens.

"Señor," he said excitedly, "señor, tell me. Can you tell me where I could find such a snake as your Chapo?"

"Sure," said the driver. "Go into the desert at the foot of the mountain called the Mountain of Red Cactus. Make sure that you go directly after a rain. As you approach the mountain, you may become frightened, thinking that someone is shooting at you with a powerful rifle. But do not be alarmed: it will be merely the chirrioneras popping their tails in an effort to dry themselves after their bath in the rain, which falls only once a year in that region."

So, when the first rain fell, old Mariano made haste into the desert and towards the Mountain of Red Cactus. Before long he stopped and listened. There came through the desert the sound as of many guns firing off. As was predicted, the old man thought of running. Surely, he thought, the bandits and the lawmen were having a terrific battle. But he remembered what the oxcart driver had told him, and went cautiously on again, approaching the foot of the mountain whence came the loud sounds of popping and cracking.

As he crept through the tall cactus and the brushy mesquite of the desert, old Mariano clasped in one hand a long pole, on the end of which was a small loop of rope made to snare with.

Slowly, slowly, he crept closer, closer to the little clearing at the foot of the mountains. Hiding behind a large stone, he watched a strange sight. Here were more than one hundred dark purple snakes, most of them popping their tails and sending little sprays of water into the air. From behind his rock Mariano arose stealthily with his long pole. But the wary snakes saw him and went squirming and bounding as fast as deer through the chaparral. All except one. A large, handsome chirrionera stayed. Not yet had he popped himself dry. He was so laden with rain water that he could move only slowly.

Upon this helpless one old Mariano pounced. Soon he had the snake's head secure in the loop at the end of the long pole. Struggle and squirm as he would, the snake could not work himself free. With a great smile on his face, the old man maneuvered the captured snake on the end of the pole through the chaparral toward his home in the little town of Venaditos.

Old Mariano turned loose the captive chirrionera in his orchard and set out for him every day a big bowl full of the finest fruit. At first the snake, on seeing the old man approach, would crawl rapidly away and cringe, coiled tightly, in the darkest corner of the orchard; but in a little time he became more tame, until soon he would eat fruit not only from the big bowl, but even out of the old man's hand.

As time passed, the creature came to feel very much at home around Mariano's house, and grew to believe, like a dog, that he was watchman of the place. Whenever a stranger came into view, the snake would stand upon his head and snap his tail so that it cracked loudly in warning. And if the old man wanted the stranger driven away, he had simply to say to the snake, "Hit him!" Then the chirrionera would race like a dark purple streak along the ground toward the one at whom his master was pointing. Standing upon his head, he would bounce around and around the victim, striking him with his tail from every direction, so that the one being beaten could only think that there were a dozen magic whips surrounding him, beating him whichever way he turned to escape.

So pleased was old Mariano with his chirrionera that he named him Angelito, which means Little Angel.

Now, careful, careful, was the sly old Mariano to keep secret from the three boys the fact that he had this Little Angel snake in his possession. The old fox waited until he had his pet trained perfectly. And then what a lashing the three fruit-stealers would get!

After some little time, one day the three boys, Juan, José, and Daniel, came carrying their ladder to old Mariano's house. Laughing and joking they came now, for they had grown to regard the old man's whippings as great sport. They were even a little disappointed that they had received no beatings for three weeks. Working leisurely, they placed their ladder in position against the wall; and Juan raised his foot to climb up.

"Hit them!"

The boys turned quickly and looked. In his door stood old Mariano, a strange smile on his face, pointing at them. At the same time, the boys caught a glimpse of a dark purple shining snake streaking toward them faster than a galloping horse. Before they could move, Angelito had circled twice around them and had dealt them each a smart blow with his tail.

Crying in surprise and pain, the three boys scattered in different directions. Angelito followed Juan and whipped him several blows. Then, streaking rapidly, rapidly, after José, the snake caught up and slapped him with his tail as he ran. The same for Daniel.

And all the while old Mariano, standing in his doorway, roared like a bear with laughter and shouted: "That's it, my precious Little Angel! Give the little devil another slap. Do not let him get away, Angelito. Ah, how does it feel? Boys, do you like this game? Very good sport, no? Oh, its funny! My stomach! I shall die of laughing."

After the dutiful Angelito had driven the three boys to their house, he came back to his violently laughing master. And late into that night, old Mariano and his chirrionera sat up, celebrating their victory. For Angelito there was a very big heap of fruit; and for the old man a bottle, some of the contents of which he poured from time to time into the gaping mouth of Angelito, who seemed greatly to relish a little stimulating drink with his meal. "My Lit-tle An-gel," old Mariano was saying in the voice of one who is talking to a little baby. "What eyes you have so beautiful! Eat much that you may have much strength to whip the little fiends hard, hard. Yes, and drink another time, my Lit-tle An-gel."

And Angelito would drink and smack his lips and say, "Ah," shaking his head, and resume eating his peaches, plums, oranges, grapes, and mangoes. "Ah, ah, smart, smart you are, my Little Angel," the old man would say, stroking the snake's head fondly. "Everything I say you understand. Drink another time, Angelito. That's it. A reward for your good work today. The thieving boys so without shame, how their hides must even now be smarting from the stinging blows you gave them. Ha! Ha! They will not visit again soon. No, no, not while you, my Little Angel, are here. Ah, how I love you, my little sweetheart, Lit-tle An-gel. Here, I give you a kiss."

For several days the three boys did not come near old Mariano's house. Very different from the feeble taps of the old man were the stout blows from Angelito's tail. Some way they must get rid of that whipping snake.

But how?

After thinking much, Juan, the eldest boy, got together in his head a plan—a plan which made him smile.

One night very dark when the moon had hid her face behind the clouds, Juan, Daniel, and José came and placed their ladder quietly against old Mariano's orchard wall. Angelito and his master were inside the house sleeping heavily after much drinking of tequila. Juan, slinging a sack over his shoulder, ascended the ladder to the top of the wall, climbed into the top of a peach tree and came down through the branches to the ground.

Peering all about him through the darkness, Juan saw over by the house something big and round. Over towards it he went, slowly, slowly feeling with his foot on the ground every step. He felt of the object. It was Angelito's bowl. And full of fruit. So considerate of his snake was old Mariano that he had prepared the night before his breakfast. Very good, thought Juan to himself. So much the better.

With his knife Juan cut open each mango, peach, and plum, and took out the seeds. Then, reaching into his sack, he got handfuls of salt, chili, and gunpowder and put a mixture of all these into the fruits where the seeds had been. When he had thus seasoned the last fruit, Juan stepped to the peach tree, climbed it to the wall, and came down the ladder.

The next morning before the sun had appeared, and while old Mariano still slumbered, out of the door toward the big bowl of fruit crawled Angelito.

In his fiery eyes was smouldering a slight ill temper—which might well be expected after such a night of drinking. Much, much hunger had Angelito. Straight to his bowl he went and began eating the fruit greedily.

Now, my friend, you know as well as I that in order for food to be savory it must be seasoned. And I can always win against the strongest garlic,

chili, or onion. But surely, anyone knows that enough is plenty. Bad enough it is to overdose food with too much of even one seasoning. But Chihuahua! Such a combination! Salt, chili, gunpowder! More dangerous this than war. One is likely to explode to all parts of the landscape, the right arm to be thrown and left hanging in a pine tree on the top of a mountain where the circling buzzards will perch and feed, the left arm to be sent sailing across the desert to land in some cactus bush about which will gather coyotes.

So greedily did Angelito begin eating that he devoured four fruits immediately. He coughed, strangled. His eyes flashed fire. Bounding into the air, he came down belching, choking, and squirming around like a rope spinning, and cracking his tail.

Cursing in his own snake language, Angelito started toward the door. In he went and jumped upon the foot of old Mariano's bed. Wrapping his neck about the foot rail, the enraged chirrionera raised his tail quivering in the air. Old Mariano lay on his face, snoring into his pillow. Down came the tail like a black flash. Whap! Old Mariano bounced up off his bed with a great yell. Sitting up, he stared with large eyes at Angelito. Down came the tail again. Whap! "Ay!" Old Mariano rubbed his eyes. Was he dreaming? Another blow from the tail assured him that he was not, and out of bed he jumped. Angelito followed and struck him a blow. Another. Another. "Ay, Angelito, have you gone crazy from so much drink last night? No, no, Angelito! This is Don Mariano, your master and friend who every day feeds you. Oh, oh, oh, poor me! Angelito, stop! You will kill me. Angelito! Angelito! Do you not recognize . . . Oh, poor me, poor me!"

Around and round the room went the old man, Angelito following him like a shadow and showering blows about his head and shoulders without stopping. Dropping to all fours, the old man crawled under the bed more rapidly than an armadillo. But there Angelito followed him. Out on the other side scrambled the old man, crying for help. From his bed he managed to grasp one of the rafters of his house and pulled himself up. Popping his tail on the ground, Angelito gave a great leap and wound himself around the rafter and beat the old man several blows. Down dropped the old man, to run around the room again, shouting, desperation in his eyes. In the corner he saw an axe. This he seized. Standing in the corner, he held the weapon over his head and shouted to Angelito, "Do not approach nearer. I will chop your fiendish head from your cursed body." With one swift flash of his tail, Angelito knocked the axe spinning from the old man's grasp.

For a moment the old man cowered trembling like a cornered rabbit. Then madly he dashed past Angelito out the door. Out sprang Angelito also, bounding along on his head behind the old man and whipping him every step with his tail. And at every blow the old man would cry out, jump, and run the faster.

Outside, near the door, stood Juan, José, and Daniel. "Just look," they called out one to the other, laughing. "Just look. How playful are the old man and his whipping snake. A game they are playing. Yes, a race. Can you believe it, the old man has regained his youth! See how lightly his feet touch the ground! See how he leaps the stones and bushes! Hurry, hurry! Little precious Angelito is catching you. Whap! Ah, the game must be tag. Whap! Another love tap! Ah, it must be that the old man also has eaten of the highly seasoned food. Look, look how playful is the little snake!"

For the greater part of a league Angelito chased old Mariano into the desert, beating the dust from his clothes at every step. Over cactus they leaped; around mesquite trees they circled; down and up the banks of creeks they fell and scrambled madly. Before their path scattered coyotes, armadillos, paisanos, rabbits, and all the other creatures of the desert, running in wild fear and confusion.

Finally, Angelito grew tired of the chase, the high seasoning having made it hard for him to fetch his breath. Back to old Mariano's house he went, and there he stayed until he and the three boys had eaten all the fruit from old Mariano's orchard. Then back he went to his home in the desert at the foot of the Mountain of Red Cactus. And not until then did old Mariano return to his house.

Today if you go to the little town of Venaditos, there you will find old Mariano. 'Is he not dead?' you ask. Ah — no, and yes. If you do not find the old man there, look nearby on the hill and about the city for an old gray burro. For old men of selfish and mean disposition do not die but turn into gray burros, which, it is will known, never die. This old burro will have no mustache to droop over his mouth, no brows to frown down over his eyes, and no sarape to pull up over his ears; so you might get from him the whole story of his life as a man.

CHARGE THIS TO THE HAT

It has been observed by some that poor men and rich men are often good friends. They stand in the shade of the mesquite and talk about the weather and the crops and the heat, but their good relationship will often turn to trouble if the poor man is thoughtless enough to bring up the subject of money. And it was just this subject of money that caused trouble between the two friends in our story.

The poor man had had very bad luck, his crops had failed, and his goats had died because they had no food. Even the poor man and his wife were beginning to go hungry. So one day the poor man said, "Wife, it isn't right that we should starve. I am going to ask our rich friend to help us." And saying this he wearily put his ragged hat upon his head and started down the dusty road towards his friend's house.

Upon reaching the rich man's home, the poor friend was received badly. He asked for food but received not so much as sympathy. In fact, the rich man was discourteous to the extent of laughing at the poor man, his attitude, and clothing, and his hat in particular.

"You need no help, my friend," said he. "Go sell your hat. As a curiosity it is worth a fortune; and it is so full of holes, it is at least a good riddle to set people guessing just when it will decide to be no hat at all."

Three years passed and the poor man's luck, which could not have been worse, was now somewhat better.

"Wife," said he, "I'm going to take the little money we have and get even with our rich friend."

First he bought himself a gray hat with a blue band; then he went to a watchmaker's shop and bought a cheap watch.

He said to the watchmaker, "I need your help. My friend, a very rich man, has insulted me and you can help me get revenge. After we have changed the price tag to indicate a very valuable timepiece, I shall leave the watch with you and call for it later. When I return you are to act as if you have never seen me before, and I shall pretend to be buying the watch for the first time. I shall take it, point to my gray hat and say, 'Charge this to the hat,' and you are to respond, 'You owe nothing; take it.'"

Being assured of the watchmaker's help, the poor man went to a jeweler, bought a string of imitation pearls, and made the same arrangements with him that he had made with the watchmaker. "When I take the pearls and say, 'Charge this to the hat,' you are to say, 'You owe me nothing; take it.'"

From the jewelry store our poor man went next to a dry goods store and bought a suit, and then to an inn, where he paid for two meals. In each case it was understood that on his return he was to point to his gray hat and say, "Charge this to the hat," instead of paying for his purchase.

With the trap well set, he visited his rich friend, and, being well-dressed, was received with great courtesy.

"My friend," said the rich man, "what a fine new hat! What kind is it?"

"Oh! it isn't so much," said the poor man; "yet it has proved valuable upon more than one occasion. However, I've come to town to make some purchases. If you don't mind, I should be pleased to have you go with me. After this business is attended to, you shall be my guest at dinner."

"With great pleasure," said the rich friend, who was much in favor of getting something for nothing. "I am pleased to accept your invitation."

They went first to the watchmaker's shop.

"Let me see a good watch," said the poor man.

"A good watch will cost a lot of money," said the merchant.

"It isn't the price; it's the watch that counts," said the customer. "I'll take that one marked three hundred dollars."

The watch was handed to the poor man.

"Charge this to the hat," said he, pointing to his gray hat.

"You owe me nothing; take it," said the merchant.

The rich friend was amazed but held his peace.

The two went immediately to the jewelry store. Here the imitation pearls had been marked up to one thousand dollars. The poor man took them and instead of paying for them said, "Charge this to the hat."

"You owe me nothing; take them," said the jeweler.

Next they entered the dry goods store and the suit was bought and paid for with a point to the hat and the words, "Charge this to the hat."

The two friends went to an inn and had dinner and from all appearances this too, like the suit, pearls, and watch, was paid for with a salute with the right hand to the gray hat and the words, "Charge this to the hat."

"What a marvelous hat!" said the rich man. "Sell it to me."

"No, my friend," said the poor man. "I could hardly live without my gray hat with the blue ribbon."

"I will give you thirty thousand dollars for it," said the rich man.

After a bit of hesitancy on the part of the poor man the deal was closed and the rich man rushed home to tell his wife.

"Woman," said he, "this is to be the day of days. Come, we will buy whatever you want."

"How?" exclaimed the wife. "You will buy the diamond necklace I asked for a year ago?"

"Certainly, woman," boasted the rich man, "and even more."

They went to the best jewelry store in town and bought a diamond necklace. Then instead of paying for it the rich friend pointed to his gray hat and said, "Charge this to the hat."

"What does that mean?" said the clerk.

"It means, stupid, that I don't have to pay for the necklace."

Evidently the clerk thought otherwise, for he had the rich man arrested.

Today, the poor man lives in luxury while the rich man is in a madhouse.

"It worked," says the rich man over and over again to anyone who will listen. "It worked; I saw it with my eyes. It is a magic hat, I tell you. The one who wears it never pays for a thing; all one needs to say is, 'Charge this to the hat.'"

THREE BITS OF ADVICE

There was once a boy who ran away from home. Though he was not a bad boy at heart, he had three habits that were by no means good. He would stick to no purpose, he was always asking about other people's affairs that did not concern him, and he would not control his temper.

Yes, my friend, this boy ran away from home, and do you know he was hardly beyond the horizon when he left the main road for a trail. He had not travelled far down this trail when he saw an old man trudging slowly towards him. Without waiting for the old man to come any closer, the boy impatiently called to him and inquired of his business, and when he did not answer, the boy flew into a rage.

Presently, however, the little old man approached him and seeing the boy's agitation, he smiled and tipped his hat. "I am a peddler of advice," he said, "Perhaps I can be of service to you."

"What kind of advice?" asked the boy.

"It will cost you one peso to find out," was the answer.

The boy had only three pesos, but curiosity induced him to give one to the little old man.

"First," said the old man, "don't leave a main road for a trail."

"Is that what you call advice?" asked the boy. "You are a fraud."

"Don't you like that one?" asked the old man. "Then give me another peso and lend an ear."

The boy reluctantly handed over the second of his three pesos and waited. "Second," said the old one, "don't ask about things that do not concern you."

"Thief," shouted the boy, "for one peso I would kill you."

"Calm yourself, my son," said the old man. "I have among my wares one more bit of advice you need. Will you buy it or not?"

The boy's curiosity was too much for him. He gave his last peso to the stranger and listened attentively for the third time.

"Don't lose your temper," laughed the old man, and before the boy could gather his wits, he had vanished into the chaparral.

Sad and with empty pockets, the youth continued on his way.

He took to the main road again just as a stranger mounted on a large black horse galloped up.

"Where to, young man?" called the stranger.

"To the city," said the boy.

"Then you need advice," responded the man. "Look, I will help you. One league up the road you will find a shortcut. You will recognize it by my horse's tracks. It will save you many miles."

The boy thanked him and continued on his journey intending to leave the main road for the path. However, never being able to keep to a purpose, he disregarded the path.

At noon he came to a ranch house. A bandit sat beneath an arbor in front of it.

"Good day, young man," he called. "You are just in time to share my dinner with me. Won't you come into the coolness of my house?" The boy entered the house and took a chair at the table. He had waited no time when a servant placed before him a dish containing the head of a man. He was at the point of asking a question when he remembered suddenly one of his three costly bits of advice. "I had better ask no questions," thought he.

"Young man," said the bandit, "what do you think of this head?"

"It is a good head," replied the boy.

"Have you no questions?" queried the bandit.

"No, señor, none."

"Would you like to see some of my keepsakes?" asked the bandit.

"If it is your pleasure to show them," said the boy, "then it will be my pleasure to see them."

A closet was opened and the boy was shown many skeletons hanging by the neck.

"How do you like my men?" asked the host.

"They are good men," answered the boy.

"Young man," said the bandit, "I kill all my guests. These men, like you, each in his turn stepped across my threshold to have dinner with me. Each was shown a head, but, different from you, they wanted to know all about it. Their curiosity brought them to their present condition. You, however, have asked nothing about things that do not concern you, and for that reason my servants will conduct you safely from the ranch. In my corral there are three mules and a horse. The mules will be loaded with gold, and the horse will be saddled. These are yours."

Six bags of gold were tied in pairs and placed on the mules. The boy mounted the horse and with the help of the servants was soon on the main road again. "Indeed," he said to himself, "it pays to keep to the main road and it pays to ask no questions about things that do not concern one. Now I am rich."

"Halt!" called a voice from the roadside, and another bandit stepped out of the chaparral and stood in the middle of the road with his arms crossed.

"What have you in those sacks?" he asked.

The boy was at the point of cursing with rage when he recalled the third bit of advice the old man had given him.

"It is a secret I prefer not to tell," he answered calmly, determined not to loose his temper.

"Speak or I shall kill you," threatened the bandit.

"If you feel that is best," said the boy, "then follow your conscience."

"Ha!" said the man, "you are a wise boy. God be with you, and may you have a pleasant journey."

After several hours of travelling the boy finally entered the city. Before many weeks had passed he had built and stocked the best store in town and was making barrels of money. Furthermore, he met and married a wealthy girl. However, the best of all was that she, too, did not leave the main road for a path, she asked no questions about things that did not concern her, and she always kept her temper.

SANDAL LEATHER

Once there were two men who lived in the small town of Coyame. One was rich and the other poor. The rich man counted his cows on an adding machine, while the poor man needed only one finger of one hand to keep track of his. Yet, Don Pedro Carrasco, the man of wealth and importance, was envious of the poor man José Días, for the latter's cow was large, fat, and never dry.

"José," said Don Pedro, "I will give you one hundred pesos for your cow."

"But, señor," said the penniless José, "she is my only possession, and if she were sold my family and I would starve without a doubt."

"I will give you ten cows in exchange for yours," said Don Pedro.

"Pardon, señor," said José, "my one cow is never dry and she gives ten times more milk than your ten cows would give."

Don Pedro walked away without further comment, but those who saw the anger in his face felt that José would soon have much cause for regret.

Three days later the two men met in the plaza of the town.

"Good day, José," said Señor Carrasco with such a show of courtesy that the penniless man was thrown completely off his guard. "Is your cheese selling well?"

"Yes, indeed," said the poor man, "with God's help I will sell enough cheese to furnish my family with food and clothing. I have no cause for complaint, thanks be to God."

"It seems a pity to spend one's life barely living, José. With sandal leather selling in Aldama at ten pesos a pair, inside two days you could be a man of wealth. You know, friend, that beyond the mountains the people have only this week learned to wear sandals. Your cow would make one hundred pairs of sandals and ten times one hundred would bring one thousand pesos. You see," continued Don Pedro, "you see, a good friend to tip one off and a bit of figuring and a bit of common sense are all one needs these days to make money out of no money at all."

"Is it really true," asked José, "that in Aldama sandals are ten pesos a pair?"

"Would I say so if they were not?" responded Don Pedro. "Go ask Lupe Aguilar, the brother-in-law of Cuca Ramírez. It was only this morning that he told me, and this very day I shall kill some cows and sell their hides for sandals."

The trick worked. Within an hour José Días was no longer content with the even trend of things. "One thousand pesos," he mused. "Just fancy, my wife could have fine clothes, the daughters the many things they need, and I would no longer have to work. A thousand pesos, just think of that." Poor José became such a victim of illusions that before nightfall he had killed his cow, skinned her, and cut the hide into small strips the size of the sole of a man's foot. Without caring for the meat in any manner, he left that very night for Aldama.

Bright and early the following morning on a street in Aldama two policemen were startled by a strange vendor's call.

"Sandals!" was the cry. "Sandals! Ten pesos a pair."

"Is he drunk or crazy?" asked one of the policemen.

"We will take him to the mayor and soon find out," said the other.

José told his story, and everyone except the mayor laughed.

"Carrasco has caused you to make a fool of yourself, my friend," said he. "Your rawhide isn't worth three pesos, much less a thousand. Here, take this coin, buy yourself a taco or two and leave Aldama."

Mechanically José accepted the gift and, without bothering to shoulder his bundle of sandal leather, took to the street.

"Now there will be no clothes for my wife," said he, "no gifts for the daughters, and now of all times there will be no rest for myself. What a fool I've been!"

Just then a street vendor called: "Masks! Devil masks!"

José turned, saw a cartload of masks, and on the very top a devil's face so red-eyed, sharp-eared, wolfish, and weird that he decided to buy it. He gave the mayor's coin to the vendor, took the mask and, placing it beneath his shirt, proceeded on his way out of town.

Night overtook him on the mountain slopes west of Coyame. With night came a cold north wind and the poor man was at the point of freezing when to the left of the road he saw a campfire. He approached it and found ten men seated on ten leather bags around the blaze.

"May I warm myself by your fire?" asked José.

A minute passed before a word was spoken. At last, however, one of the men told him to come near the fire and make himself comfortable.

José was too cold just then to care who his hosts might be. Later, however, while warming his hands in the blaze, he studied them one by one and concluded that they were bandits.

Suddenly a noise was heard. The men jumped to their feet.

"What is it?" asked José.

"One of the saddle horses staked in the brush," said the leader. "We thought it might be Indians. A tribe has been on our trail since sunrise."

José figured it would be well to leave, but the warmth of the fire and the rushing of the bitter norther through the cats-claw brush, plus the fact that he was very tired, caused him to delay and finally to abandon any intention of leaving the fire for the night.

One after the other the bandits spread their sarapes side by side near the fire, lay down, and went to sleep. The night grew colder and the wind stronger. José was too busy keeping warm to think of sleep. For an hour he spent the time turning first his face and then his back to the fire. He got more wood from the brush, built a larger blaze, and still he thought that surely his nose would freeze.

He was warming his back and wondering just how he could make himself more comfortable when suddenly he remembered the mask. He placed it over his face. His nose, ears, and cheeks soon were warm again but his hands were cold. He turned to the fire, reached into the blaze and was rubbing his hands and groaning when the bandit nearest the blaze awoke.

Now, this fellow hadn't been a good man and what he saw looking at him through the flames and smoke paralyzed him with fear. Presently he eased over to the nearest bandit and touched him with his elbow. This fellow also, like the first, was scared stiff by what he saw and could hardly breathe. One by one the bandits awoke until the last man, the leader, was nudged by his neighbor.

Now the leader had been having a bad dream. He dreamed he was dead, and the devil had come to get him. When he awoke to find this terrible face staring at him through the fire, he screamed in terror and dragging his sarape behind him, he ran into the darkness yelling, "Run men! Run for your lives!"

José was unaware that they were awake until he saw them running away and heard the captain screaming at the top of his voice for his men to run. "Indians!" he thought and followed hot on the heels of the bandits. One of them saw him coming and yelled, "He's coming, men! Run faster!"

José ran so fast the mask slipped over his eyes and he stumbled and fell to the ground. He lost no time in getting to his feet again, but he had lost his sense of direction for the moment. He listened. There was no sound anywhere.

"Strange," said he as he fumbled the mask. "Strange. I wonder why they . . . " And then he remembered the devil's mask. "It must have been the mask. I must call these fellows back and explain."

He followed in the direction they had fled until he came to a large precipice, and there a hundred feet below he heard a bandit groaning. They had all fallen over the cliff and were dead or dying.

José returned to the fire and picked up one of the ten leather pouches. Greatly to his surprise it was full of gold pieces. He opened another. It, too, was full of gold; and so it was with the rest of them—all full of gold. He tied the pouches in pairs and put them on five of the saddle horses that had been staked by the bandits. Then mounting another horse, he set out for his hut and, with the ten sacks of gold all safe, reached it before dawn.

At ten o'clock that morning the one old gossip of the little town of

Coyame came nosing around José's hut.

"Good morning, José," he said.

"Good morning, señor."

"They tell me you killed your cow, my friend."

"Oh, yes! I killed her."

"They tell me, José, that you tried to sell her hide for sandal leather at ten pesos a pair," added the gossip smiling at the trick that had been played on José.

"Look, my friend," said José. "Don Pedro Carrasco did me a great injustice."

"You don't say," said the man.

"Yes," continued José, "he told me to sell the hide at ten pesos a pair, but fortunately I met a friend in Aldama who tipped me off to the fact that sandal leather was selling at twenty pesos a pair. Look."

He took a handful of gold from his right pocket. "What do you think of that?" he said with a wee small hint of boasting. "And if that isn't convincing, look."

He drew another handful of gold from his left pocket.

"Look," he went on, "this is yours. Take it. Certainly, all of it, my friend. Only do me one little favor. Don't tell Don Pedro Carrasco about it. I am going to buy his cows, kill them all and sell their hides. Think of it; at twenty pesos a pair for sandals, with all those cows I shall soon be the richest man in the whole republic. But remember, not a word to Don Pedro Carrasco."

What were promises to the town's gossip? Within thirty minutes Don Pedro knew the whole story. By nightfall he had killed all his cows and at dawn the following morning he was in Aldama with the first wagonload of sandal leather.

"Sandals!" he cried, "Sandals! Twenty pesos a pair."

"Listen," said one of the policemen to the other. "He's back again."

"No," responded the other officer, "it's someone else."

"Is he drunk or crazy?" asked the first.

"Crazy, likely, and twice as crazy as the other. Let's take him to the mayor."

Don Pedro told his story and everyone laughed, including the mayor. In fact the mayor laughed himself into a fit of coughing and it was some time before he could regain enough composure and dignity to speak as an impartial judge.

"An old proverb says that 'We all go limping, each on his own foot,'" said the mayor to Don Pedro. "That is to say that if we act foolishly it is because of our own faults. And you, Don Pedro, have limped into a bad business because you were greedy. Your sin carries its own penitence. And since justice was so prompt in this case I feel there is nothing for me to do except to give you your liberty and a bit of good advice. Remember this: The way to pay is to return the favor. Give my regards to your friend José Días, and on your way back home you might try singing a song to keep from crying."

José and his family are wealthy now and they have given much money to the saints of the Church and to the poor.